ROBINSON CALCULATOR

Paul Levinson

Connected Editions

1

I first noticed the name on a headstone in the Woodlawn Cemetery in the Bronx – "Robinson Calculator".

I mean, would they be so blatant – to bury one of their own under a tombstone which plainly identified the deceased as "Calculator"? That would bring hiding in plain sight to a whole new level.

I'm not making this up. You'd see this with your own eyes if you were in the right spot in the cemetery. I'd understand if you didn't – most people are only visiting the cemetery because they're grieving for a loved one. But sometimes there's less grief than other times – you know, for a member of the family by marriage, and you didn't really know the old guy all that well. And if there were no tears in your eyes, and you looked in the right place – trust me, you'd see that name incised in stone, too. "Robinson Calculator".

I've been tracking those people for years – though, obviously, they're not really people. And the sight of that name on the headstone was a shard of ice in my heart. Because it meant they didn't care anymore, didn't worry about who saw them or knew about them.

***

I have nothing against them. In fact, I like them – they have spunk and style. My friend – a college buddy – had been married to one. That was the only reason I knew about them. Most people had no idea Calculators even existed. Dave's wife didn't use her maiden name.

I chuckled to myself. "Maiden" doesn't seem quite right for a Calculator, does it? Doesn't seem quite right for anyone anymore, but I liked this particular Calculator – hell, more than that, I'd wanted her. I'd been very attracted to her. I had mixed feelings when they broke up. Dave and Lianne had planned on adopting, but he had become increasingly obsessed with seeing his DNA come to life in a new being, and of course there was no way that could happen with Lianne.

I had been on the verge of contacting her a bunch times in the few years since they'd split, but seeing that name on the headstone gave me new impetus.

***

Just to be clear, I know that people have all kinds of last names derived from real objects, and I don't think for a minute that the holders of names derived from objects are endowed with the physical properties of those objects. I mean, no one looked for gold or water when they saw Barry Goldwater – though for all I knew, he sported a gold ring or watch, and his body was certainly made of whatever big percentage of water, like all human beings.

Hey, there was a girl by the name of Samantha Sugar in my high school bio class, and I surely didn't think she was literally sweet – though she did have a sweet smile when she wanted to show it and a sweet ass, too, in those snug cotton jeans.

But the Calculators were something else. The name apparently originated in Europe, as far back as the Golem and the real automata that preceded the mythical Golem by centuries. Heron of ancient Alexandria had constructed automata far earlier, though there is no surviving evidence that he called them Calculator as a last name, or anything at all. They mostly had only one name back then, anyway, right?

But the Calculators were different. Whenever they originated, they started "life" as a family, a big family, with aunts and uncles as well as parents and children. And the family grew. With first and last names, and the last name was always Calculator.

***

I texted Lianne Calculator. "How are you doing?"

"Wow! Wild to hear from you! I'm watching *Battlestar Galactica.* Never gets old," she replied.

Figured. I caught my breath. I was surprised by how good it felt to be in touch with her again. "Hey, how about lunch in the next few days – Blue Ribbon Sushi on Sullivan Street?" I knew she lived in the Village and worked from home. I also knew Dave hated sushi and she loved it.

"Sure," she replied. "How does Thursday sound to you?"

***

I ordered the big orange clam and she ordered the sweet ebi. We talked for a few minutes about inconsequential things.

Then she took my hand. "I'm not ready yet for anything more than friendship."

"Ok."

"I know you're the kind of guy who thinks if she doesn't want my dick she doesn't want my soul, but–"

My mouth hung open. I filled it with a piece of clam. I guess that's what I meant by spunk.

"Do you think I have a soul?" she shifted focus. "Seriously."

"In a religious sense?" I sipped some sencha tea, grateful for the change of topic. "I'm not sure I know what that means. If it's something that God supposedly breathed into human beings, well, then I'm agnostic. If it's just a word for what my brain

3

contains, then, yeah, I think you're my mental equal. I wouldn't think you were any different from me at all, if your name were not ..."

"Calculator?"

"Right," I said. "Why do you use it?"

"It's the law," Lianne replied.

I laughed. "What law would that be? The politicos know about you?"

"Common law," Lianne said. "Goes back centuries."

"Ah, ok – so it's some kind of profound, deeply embedded custom."

She gave me a look. "I don't know if I'd call it 'profound'." She bit into one of the crunchy fried shells of her shrimp, which had been served to her so quickly that its appearance on our table almost seemed surreptitious.

"But it's an important custom," I said.

She nodded and crunched away.

"Who came up with it – was it imposed on you?" I asked her.

She cleared her palate and throat with tea. "We did ... why are you suddenly so interested?"

I told her about Robinson Calculator in the cemetery.

"Never heard of him," she said and summoned the waiter. "I'll have another ebi."

"I'm fine," I said to the waiter. And to Lianne, "Do you know all the Calculators?"

Now she laughed. "Of course not. Do you know all the human beings?" Her laughter sounded like rain. I like rain. That Beatles song has always been one of my favorites. I sang a bar of "Rain" under my breath. I'd heard it just yesterday on Peter Asher's show on Sirius XM Radio.

"I assume there aren't as many Calculators as humans, right?" I said and summoned another waiter. "More tea please." I looked at Lianne, who nodded. "For both of us."

The waiter quickly bowed and left.

"No, we aren't as numerous as humans," Lianne said, in slow, mockingly exaggerated tones. "But I doubt you know anything close to the names of every human even in your neighborhood or on your block."

I nodded.

"And the only reason you know about me – about my kind – is I was married to Dave," Lianne added.

The original waiter returned with Lianne's ebi and a pot of tea. He refilled our cups. "Anything more?" he asked, politely.

I shook my head no. "When do you think your people made a decision to put one of their names on such a publicly viewable tombstone?" I asked Lianne.

She considered for a moment. "I don't know that they did. I mean, I believe you about what you saw on that tombstone, but I don't know if that was the result of a decision by the Calculators."

"I took a picture of it," I said and reached for my phone.

"I believe you," Lianne said again.

"Ok," I said, and looked down for a moment at my tea. The pale green liquid seemed to shimmer in my cup, as if, I don't know, in response to some soft sound wave. Then I realized there was indeed sound in the room, or at least at our table. Lianne was singing. And she was somehow singing all the parts to the song, all the harmony, so softly that only I could hear.

I looked around at the people at the other tables. They couldn't hear her. It was like I was wearing earbuds and Lianne was in the phone. It was beautiful. B. J. Thomas's "Rock 'n' Roll Lullaby". She was singing it just for me.

My father had loved that song, especially those Blossom and Beach Boy harmonies. He had sung more than half of those harmonies as we walked the beach on the bay side of Cape Cod. I knew I'd never told Lianne about that – hell, I doubt I ever told Dave.

Lianne smiled at me and stopped singing. "I researched you.

"After I texted you about lunch?"

"After the first time I met you, when I was with Dave," she replied.

Now *I* smiled. She was very distracting. "You think human beings put the name Calculator on that headstone?" I asked her. I wanted to stay focused.

Lianne sucked on her ebi sushi. Her eyes closed in appreciation. She sang the chorus almost in a whisper.

She obviously didn't want to discuss this. I sipped my tea.

"It began to become public in the 1920s," Lianne suddenly said. "It all began to change with *R.U.R.*"

"Karol Čapek's play? *Rossum's Universal Robots*?"

"Yeah," Lianne said. "That's when robots first entered the popular culture in a big way – got Asimov going, and Data, and *Westworld* and everything else. Čapek gave robots their name."

"Did Čapek know about you?" I asked.

"About the Calculators? I don't know – I wasn't alive back then."

It occurred to me that I knew nothing about Calculator lifespans. "How old are you? I mean–"

She squeezed my hand. I had touched her hand before, and I knew it was warm, but for some reason I was a little surprised by its warmth now anyway.

"I enjoyed this," she said and stood. "How much do I owe you?" She fished for her phone.

The waiter had yet to bring the bill. "On me," I said. "But– I hope I didn't offend you with anything I said–"

"You didn't," she said, and leaned over and kissed me on the lips to prove it. I believed her, and thought, well, Dave was even more of a fool than I'd thought he'd been to leave her.

I watched her walk to the front of the restaurant. If it walks like a duck and talks like a duck ... well, she sure walked like a woman.

***

I paid the bill and took the D train up to Central Park. Walking in the park helped me think.

The key point in understanding Lianne and her people – yeah, they seemed like people to me, even though I knew that technically they weren't – was that they had been around a long time. Our digital age and the decades before get all the credit – at least the public credit – for robots and AI. And Alexa and Siri and all of that are indeed 21st century. But Charles Babbage had started it all back in the 1820s, with his Difference Engine. And that was more than just a fanciful design – a working Difference Engine had actually been constructed at the Science Museum in London around 1990, if memory served.

So Babbage's designs worked, at least for very primitive computer calculators. Could they have been responsible for the Calculators – or someone building off his work, like Ada Lovelace? Had they given the name Calculator to an actual body made of flesh and blood and some sort of primitive electric circuitry? Well, according to Lianne Calculator, no, the Calculators existed long before Babbage. Could I believe her about that? If she was telling the truth, the Calculators likely had happened the other way around, with Babbage and Lovelace jumping on the work of someone else, some "mute, inglorious Milton" of computing, as my favorite line in that sad Thomas Gray poem had it about geniuses who died without ever achieving any notice or fame. Except this Milton likely had lived long before the real John Milton and his *Paradise Lost*.

But if the Calculators owed their origin to someone else, then whom? Some person, or going further back, some civilization that left no other traces of its existence, or none that we knew of?

Yeah, walks in the park helped me think. Sometimes too much.

2

It was time to see Dave. He was the best source that I knew, other than Lianne herself, with detailed knowledge of the Calculators. And, given that Lianne seemed to have an agenda of some sort all her own, Dave could be helpful.

He was easy enough to find and meet. He was a Professor of Philosophy at the New School, down on 14th Street in the north end of the Village.

I texted him with a lunch invitation. It felt a little weird, proposing lunch with Dave the day after lunch with his ex-wife Lianne, but I didn't feel like waiting, and the weirdness still would have been there a week or a month from now.

"Sure," Dave replied. "I'm at Bobst Library, doing some research. It's at NYU, off Washington Square Park. You know where that is, right?"

"I do."

"How about we meet out front in two hours – around 1pm?"

"Great," I said. "See you then."

Dave was like that. First time we'd been in touch in several years, and he says sure, just like that. Well, we'd studied philosophy together on the other side of the pond over at the London School of Economics, and that kind of experience can bond you for life.

***

I walked up to meet him in front of Bobst at the appointed time. The New School and NYU had reciprocal library privileges once again, if I remembered correctly. Fordham University, where I taught up in the Bronx, did not. On the other hand, we had a pretty deep and well-stocked library, still a great resource, even in this digital age, with a fair number of books from the last two centuries that had not yet been scanned and put online.

Dave looked pretty much the same as the last time I'd seen him, a tad more paunchy, and grey in his hair.

"Jonathan," he clapped me on the back and shook my hand, "you look exactly the same."

"You too! What's your pleasure for lunch?"

"How about Blue Ribbon Sushi – about a five-minute walk from here, on the other side of Houston Street."

I'd learned a long time ago there was no point in fighting coincidence, if that's what this was. "Sure."

We walked a few steps. "Would you believe I had lunch in that very same restaurant with Lianne just yesterday?" I said to Dave.

"Really? Yes, I'd believe it – she's crazy about sushi," Dave said. "Ironically, I developed a taste for it myself after our divorce.... What are you, making some kind of movie about us for that film and philosophy class you were teaching, and this is your research?" He laughed.

Good to see he wasn't angry. "You know me too well! I've actually been thinking about doing that, and I now have a connection at Netflix. But you know I've always been interested in the Calculators. And I saw a name, 'Robinson Calculator,' carved on a headstone, plain as day, a few days ago at Woodlawn Cemetery in the Bronx."

"Hmm, that *is* interesting," Dave said. "When I was with Lianne, they made a big deal about staying off the radar."

"Exactly," I said. "That's why I found the tombstone so unusual." I showed him the picture on my phone.

He looked at it carefully. "First time I've ever seen anything like that."

***

We reached the restaurant. The hostess recognized me and beamed, apparently honored that I'd come back the very next day for another lunch.

I was glad to see the orange clam was still on the "specials" menu. I ordered it again. As I used to tell my ex-wife, when I find something I like, I stick with it.

Dave looked at me and ordered the same. Our tea arrived.

"You know, probably the main reason we broke up is Lianne always felt I was studying her, even in bed." He sipped his tea and shook his head.

"Were you?" I might as well see where this went, if he was raising the subject.

"Of course. Wouldn't you? Isn't that why you're here?"

I answered bluntness with bluntness. "What is she made of, inside? If you don't mind my asking. I mean, did you ever see any x-rays or body scans of her?"

"She stayed strictly away from doctors," Dave replied. "For obvious reasons."

I nodded. "She never got sick?"

"She had some allergies in the summer. A cold every once in a while," Dave said. "But nothing that ever drove her to seek medical attention – as far I know. We were only married for three-and-a-half years."

Our food arrived. I shook my head a little, in disbelief. "How did they have the knowledge back then to create someone like

Lianne?"

Dave was a philosopher. I knew he welcomed such questions.

"I honestly don't know," he said. "She refused to ever talk about it. And I couldn't find anything in any research. "But … "

Our waiter returned with a teapot. "More tea?"

"Yes," Dave said. He seemed glad to be interrupted.

"And?" I prodded. I wasn't about to let tea change the topic.

Dave sipped his refilled cup. "And, I don't know, I guess I wouldn't be totally shocked to find out that Lianne is as human as you or I, and the whole Calculator thing is some kind of hoax."

***

I took my phone out of my pocket and showed him the photo again. "You think that's a hoax?" I also thought about that multiple harmony she had sung for me in this very place, just yesterday, but, I don't know, it felt too personal for me to mention to him.

He barely glanced at the photo this time. "All that proves is that someone by the name of Robinson Calculator is buried there. It doesn't prove that he was some kind of android or robot or artificially constructed human, or that Lianne actually is, too."

"No, of course not," I said. "But what's the likelihood of my seeing that, out of the blue, years after knowing about you and Lianne, and what you were sure Lianne really was, at least then?"

Dave shook his head and said nothing.

I hadn't expected this.

He dug into his clam. I did the same. No point in pressing the conversation, in probing his literally intimate knowledge of Lianne any further, if it made him so uncomfortable. Maybe I'd been wrong to push it this far.

"You should talk to the blind professor," Dave eventually said.

"He's a bit of a Brooklyn hipster but a specialist on everything from the Golem to the Frankenstein monster."

***

I caught up with Professor Rodney Rodriguez – Dave's "blind professor" – at a science fiction convention the following week in Westchester County. He wore thick dark glasses and was, indeed, blind. Appropriately, he was introducing a 1920 movie of *The Golem – Der Golem, wie er in die Welt kam* – "The Golem, as he came into the world". Joe Rapsis, a musician from Bedford, New Hampshire, provided musical effects on a keyboard. With all of my focus on names these days, I wondered if he was also into rap music.

Rodriguez provided a vivid and knowledgeable context for the film. His body shook as he talked, and somehow that seemed totally apt and natural. "The essence of the Golem, and of all its predecessors and successors, is life from non-life. The original Adam was a kind of golem, right? He was created from dust. The Golem of Chelm from the late 1500s was created from some kind of inanimate matter. The famous Golem of Prague a few years later was made from clay – he is the basis of our movie tonight. But speaking of Prague, it's no coincidence that Karel Čapek, a Czech, wrote *R. U. R.* in 1920. And Asimov's robots followed some twenty years later – all life from nonlife."

"I thought the robot stories are about artificial intelligence, not artificial life," some guy with unkempt long grey hair who looked like a golem himself called out from the front row, though no one had called for questions.

"The two go hand in hand in robots," Rodriguez replied, pleased to get the comment. "Robots move through the world – they're not disembodied brains in a vat or programs in a computer. They're intelligent because they're alive. That's why they're a kind of golem."

I figured what the hell and raised my own hand. Then I realized

Rodriguez couldn't see it. "Is there any indication of who created the golem in his various forms," I asked. "We know that Asimov's robots were invented by his character Susan Calvin, right?"

"Good question," Rodriguez replied. "The golems were created by rabbis – but their creation was more an act of magic than science or invention. By the way, Čapek 's robots were created from organic material, and were more like androids than robots – they could pass for strange humans, and didn't look like machines."

I hadn't known that. So the Calculators – Lianne, Robinson, and however many there were – were like the Čapek robots which predated Asimov's. And if they were even older, as Lianne had said, that meant that maybe Čapek knew about them, and had based his robots on the Calculators.

***

I stopped in Dobbs Ferry on the way home, to pick up a belt that I'd left in a shoe-repair shop. The loop needed repair, and I'd also needed some new holes punched into the belt, to accommodate the pounds I'd taken off, swimming at the New York Sports Club every day.

Something about this shop, I realized as I walked in, felt like it had relevance to the Calculators, even though I'd brought my belt into this place at least a week or more before I'd seen Robinson Calculator carved on the gravestone in the cemetery.

I'd actually almost forgotten about my belt – it had likely been ready since before the cemetery. I thought of that old joke and laughed to myself: A guy goes back to his old neighborhood, sees the old shoe-repair shop still in business on the corner. He walks into the shop, and the proprietor, some elderly craftsman from Italy or wherever, looks at him, walks into the back, comes out with a pair of shoes the visitor left in the store twenty or thirty years earlier and never picked up. Well, I hadn't waited that long, and the proprietor here was a Mr. Chen, but that's what this felt like.

Chen nodded, walked into the back of his shop, and returned a few long moments later with my belt. "I also sewed, it was coming loose," he said and pointed to the sewing on the edges of the belt. "No charge!"

"Thank you," I replied and left the store. I'd already paid for the repair – four dollars, believe it or not – and I didn't want to insult the generosity of his sewing gift by insisting on paying for it. Ok, Chen and this kind of repair shop did have some relevance to my Robinson Calculator obsession. Given their antiquity, it was clear that the Calculators didn't emerge from some laboratory or assembly line. They no doubt were the product of craftsmen, tinkerers like Edison, like Mr. Chen, who took personal pride in their work.

Well, that's not to say that laboratory scientists don't take pride in what they do, and Thomas Edison was certainly not from antiquity or the Middle Ages, but there was something about the Calculators that whispered the pleasure of someone creating a lifelike statue out of stone or wood. Except the Calculators were more than lifelike. They were life, definitely some kind of life.

I decided on impulse to text Lianne again. I would never say she was lifelike. She was straight-up alive. Vibrantly living her life. I suddenly got what Dave had been trying to tell me. No craftsman or scientist could have made her. If anything, she was more the product of some insanely powerful magic, like the Golem. But that didn't seem like an explanation for her existence, either – or not an explanation I was inclined to accept. It certainly wouldn't play as well as secret science in the movie I was indeed thinking more and more about making.

I needed to know Lianne better – I needed to know what Dave had known. She had told me point blank that she didn't want anything more than friendship between us, right now, but—

"How about dinner, this time?" I messaged her.

"Love to," she replied instantly. "When and where?"

***

We met at the Lido Restaurant in Harlem three nights later. Sushi wasn't the only food I liked, and she apparently felt the same way.

I got the warm kale salad with shrimp, she got the duck something or other. We talked about superficial things, just as we had at the start of the last meal we'd shared. This was all my fault, this time, not hers. I was relishing the normal banter and the dinner too much to spoil it with questions about the nature of her existence.

We finished the first bottle of wine before dessert. I asked her if she wanted more.

She smiled and shook her head no. "You're wondering if alcohol affects Calculators the same as humans, right?"

"No, I was just asking—"

"It does--," Lianne began, just as the waiter approached and asked if we wanted another bottle of wine.

"No," we both turned and began, and Lianne's elbow tipped over a full glass of water, a glass with a very thin stem.

"Not to worry," the waiter said, and went off to get some napkins.

The water was all over the table and Lianne's lap. Ever the gentleman, I started patting the table dry, while Lianne patted her lap. *You're wondering if we rust*, I heard her say in my mind's ear, *well we don't*. In reality, she laughed, a really nice laugh, and said, "I'm such a klutz."

"No, you're not," I said, and looked up from the table to her lips, and kissed them.

She kissed me back and twirled her tongue around mine. "Our kind lies, too," she said, when we came up for air. "And we change our minds."

The waiter approached with napkins.

"We're ok," I told him.

"Like when I said I didn't want to be more than friends," she finished her thought, softly.

"Would you like the dessert menu?" the waiter asked.

I looked at Lianne. "We'll take the check," I told the waiter.

***

We Ubered up to my apartment in Inwood.

"Nice view of the river," Lianne said, but that was the last we looked out of the window that evening.

I'm not sure if it was the best sex I ever had, but it was right up there. These things are non-comparable, anyway.

"I love you," I almost said. I was sure I hadn't actually said that, and yet—

"The testicles of the male quail are twice the size of its heart," Lianne murmured.

And she soon was asleep on my chest, softly snoring.

I gently stroked her back, and tried to make some sense of this. I kept coming back to what Dave had implied. What difference did it make, whether she was human, or somehow constructed to be indistinguishable from a human in all important ways, maybe in all ways.

Well, not in every way. I didn't have to worry about using a condom, or asking her if she was on some kind of birth control.

But that wasn't a defining characteristic of every human, either – there were, after all, some women who couldn't get pregnant, some men and some women who couldn't conceive.

She'd come, twice. I liked the sound of her voice like that. It was as human as it came.

What if the only significant difference between Calculators and humans was that humans constantly wondered about the humanlike characteristics of Calculators – how they were just like us, how they were very different from us?

I fell asleep with Lianne in my arms, thinking about her face, not my movie.

***

I awoke the next morning. Lianne was gone. She'd left a note on her pillow, like in a dozen television shows.

"Had a great time," the note said. "Had an early appointment. Let's do again."

It occurred to me that I had no idea what Lianne did – I knew she worked at home, but I had never talked to her or Dave about what that work was. In all of our conversations, in all of my questions about who or what she essentially was, what she did for a living hadn't come up.

I decided to take a walk in the park – this time, Inwood Hill Park, a few feet from my apartment building. Yeah, I hadn't yet lost faith in the ability of walks in the park to help me think. The sun was bright, and the air was rich with late Spring pollen. Fortunately, I wasn't allergic. It was all good.

I was a professor of philosophy and a filmmaker, but also an amateur historian. Maybe not so amateur. The history of knowledge, an intrinsic part of epistemology, was inevitably a study of history, too.

I and many others had always wondered about the spark that had gotten our civilization going. The Chinese, the Arabs, many cultures had made great discoveries, and accomplished great things. But there was something about the Greek and Roman combination that had ultimately ignited the science and technology that had lifted us off this planet, had cracked the code of life, and, yeah, had created apps which certainly had a lot of the characteristics of human intelligence – apps that answered questions, provided instructions, apps you could practically fall in love with, if you weren't careful.

And Lianne had presumably come out of that human mode of invention – unless the Chinese or some other non-Greco-Roman civilization had some incredible expertise in flesh-and-blood artificial intelligence that had been hidden from the rest of the world.

But maybe there was another way of looking at this – could Lianne and the Calculators have come not from the distant past but the distant or not-so-distant future? That would explain why we had no knowledge of who created the Calculators – how could we have knowledge of circumstances of creation which hadn't happened yet?

But that possibility – that the Calculators had come here to our past from our future – required time travel. And travel to the past engendered paradoxes which were far more insurmountable than the unaccountable existence of human-like androids. If I traveled to the past to change something and changed it, how would I have had the knowledge of what to change in the first place? The multi-worlds hypothesis, that every time the time-traveler changed something in the past, a new world was brought into being, could help at least a little with that problem. Jonathan1 from World1 travels to the past and changes something. This brings into being World2, where that event didn't happen, and Jonathan2 had no knowledge of it. So there's no paradox, because the time traveler was Jonathan1 not Jonathan2. A cool way of getting out of the paradox, but, let's face it, a new world coming into being with every drop of the time traveler's hat was a state of affairs even more incredible than time travel itself.

And time travel to the future had its own set of crazy issues. If I traveled to tomorrow and was lucky enough to see Lianne in those same lavender panties she'd had on last night, did that mean she'd have no choice tomorrow but to wear those lavender panties? What if black was her preference tomorrow morning? What happened to her free will?

Ok, so Lianne coming from the future might remove the questions of what kind of civilization created her in the past, and how come we didn't know about it, but coming from the future saddled us with problems that were far worse.

I looked across the Hudson at the Palisades. There was a theory floating around – not really a theory, more like pure speculation – that the Palisades had been carved whole out of the rocks by some alien civilization from the stars. Could the Calculators be the result of some alien visitation to Earth, eons ago?

Well, that would explain why there was no known human civilization with that kind of technology, but what other evidence did we have of such an alien visitation?

There was a professor in the Comm Department at Fordham – Kathleen Harney – who had some expertise in that area. She'd given a paper a few years ago at a faculty seminar on the correlation between intensity of religious belief and belief in UFOs, and had found in her surveys, I guess surprisingly, that fundamentalists were more likely to believe in extraterrestrials than were atheists, agnostics, and people with casual religious beliefs. I rarely if ever attended those seminars – a colleague in my department had twisted my arm to come and hear this – but I'd really enjoyed Harney's presentation—

My phone beeped with a text. It was from Lianne. "U up for lunch today? Someone I'd like u to meet. I saw a nice-looking restaurant around the corner from your apartment building."

3

The Indian Road Café was much better than it should have been. Located on the ground floor of a big old shapeless apartment building that took up most of the block, much like mine, just a few steps from mine. But its food and drink were delicious – a little American, a little Japanese, a little this and that – and Inwood Hill Park was right across the street.

I got to the Café around 5 minutes to 1pm – about 5 minutes earlier than our arranged meeting time, unusual for me. I looked around the Café and breathed in the usual welcome aromas, mostly coffee with a hint of some kind of liqueur. Lianne was not yet here, but a man caught my eye. He half stood, and waved me over to his table.

He looked something like Timothy Leary, with long, slightly messy, white and grey hair. (If you don't know what that looks like, look him up on Google.)

"Jonathan?" he said to me, and gestured to a chair. The table seated four.

I obliged and took a seat. "I assume you're the one Lianne wanted me to meet?"

He nodded and sipped a beer. It was light, but otherwise, I'm no expert on beer.

"And you are?" I asked.

A waiter came by. "What are you drinking?" he asked me.

"Iced tea," I replied.

"Ok," the waiter said. "Ready to order?" he asked me and included 'Timothy' in his question.

"We're expecting one more person," I replied.

"Lianne won't be coming," 'Timothy' said.

"What?" I asked sharply, confused and not happy.

The waiter started to ask us again if we were ready to order but thought the better of it. "I'll come back in a few minutes for your order. Would you like another one?" he asked my companion, who had emptied his mug.

"I'm fine, thanks," he replied.

The waiter nodded and walked away.

"What do you mean, she's not coming?" I demanded, in a quiet voice that barely concealed my displeasure.

"She had an unexpected engagement," 'Timothy' replied.

"Where?"

"I don't know," 'Timothy' said, and raised his hands in a soothing gesture.

I didn't buy it. "And you are?" I repeated my earlier question, unanswered due to the waiter's arrival.

"Unimportant," he said.

So my question would have been unanswered in any case. "Look—" I began.

"I know," he said, "you came here to see Lianne."

"Right," I said, and looked at my phone. I began to text her.

"She's not likely to answer you," 'Timothy' replied.

I messaged her anyway, and stared at the phone, waiting for her reply. I got nothing. I couldn't even be sure, with this phone, if she'd received my text.

The waiter came by with my tea.

"We still need a few more minutes," 'Timothy' informed him.

"Of course," the waiter said, and walked away.

"I assure you, she's fine," the man across the table told me, anticipating my question.

But I wasn't reassured in the slightest. "Look—" I began again.

"My last name is Calculator," he interrupted me, again. "And my first name is John. Does that help put you at ease?"

"No, not really," I replied. "John is probably the most common name in the English language. It's practically my name, too." Not to mention that he'd just said he was a Calculator.

John laughed. It wasn't as melodic as Lianne's. "I can't help what my name is," he said. "I didn't choose it."

"Who did?"

"Long story," John said, "and I don't want to take up too much of your time. Let me tell you why I wanted to meet you. You're very interested in the Calculators, I know. You think you saw a name on a tombstone—"

"I don't think that, I know that," I said, with some heat now, and went to my photos on my phone. "What the hell—" The photo of the tombstone was gone. Could this John have somehow erased it, as I was sitting here word-sparring with him?

"Let me be brief," John said. "I know you like Lianne, and she likes you. But this is not a good time for the two of you ... to get involved. Take my advice. Back off. Let this breathe. You're both young, there'll be plenty of time for the two of you later."

"Who exactly are you, her father?"

John smiled wanly, reached into his wallet, and stood, He put a 20-dollar bill on the table. "This should cover our beverages."

"Are you a Calculator leader?" I asked him.

"Give it time. Trust me. You'll get the answers you seek." And he walked towards the door.

"Ready to order now?" our waiter returned and asked.

"This will be it," I replied and gestured to the twenty dollars on the table. "Keep the change."

I walked quickly to the door, intending to catch up with John. But three mothers with twice as many little kids were entering the café at just that moment.

I got outside a few crucial seconds later. I looked in every direction. There was no sign of John.

***

I half ran to the elevated train on Broadway. I could take that to 242nd Street in the Bronx, and Uber from there to Woodlawn Cemetery.

The train took longer than usual to arrive, the clanking on the tracks was painfully slow, and even the Uber took twice as long as indicated to pick me up. Nothing was going right for me today.

I eventually got to the cemetery. I knew exactly where the Robinson Calculator tombstone was located. I walked there as quickly as I could without attracting attention.

Easy enough to take another photo of that tombstone, as many pics as I wanted. Whatever or whoever had erased my first photo had also deleted it from my cloud. I realized that this could have been Lianne's handiwork, when I was blissfully unconscious last night. I really preferred not to think that. But I hadn't a clue about how John might have managed to do it. If it indeed had been him – if he had somehow erased my photo on my phone and on my cloud when I'd been sitting there, furious that Lianne was not there, not paying any attention at first to my phone – then this bespoke powers of the Calculators I'd never heard of or thought about. But

I still wanted to believe it was not Lianne, setting me up with great sex, taking advantage when I was sound asleep beside her.

I saw the tombstone in the distance. I could see immediately that there would be no photo today. And, I had a sinking feeling, on any day. The tombstone was draped, and two men were busily at work on it, in what appeared to be some kind of sandblasting action.

I approached them as non-aggressively as I could. A third man approached us from the side. Some kind of security. "Please, sir," he said to me, in an Eastern European accent, "let the men work. Do not disturb them. We always must have respect for the dead."

They were erasing what was on that tombstone. Robinson Calculator. I couldn't let them do that. I spoke up: "I'm a member of the family. Robinson's son. We didn't give you permission to do that." I took a step closer.

The security guard did the same. We were face to face. "You have identification, please?"

"Sure," I made a point of fumbling with my wallet. I could rush the tombstone, brush aside the drapery, and photograph whatever was still left on it—

But I saw two cops out of the corner of my eye, leisurely walking in our direction. Whether they were here to grieve, or on routine patrol, or as additional security, I had no way of knowing. My security guard saw where I was looking, turned to look at the police, then turned back to me. "You have identification?" he said to me again.

The sandblasting continued. If I pushed past the guard to get to the tombstone, I'd definitely be arrested, likely for assault. That wouldn't do me or my quest the slightest good.

The sandblasting stopped. The workers removed the drape. Just as I'd feared. There was now no lettering at all on the smooth, gleaming face of the tombstone. Just some residual dust.

I sighed and backed off. "I must've forgotten it, left it at home," I said quickly, and turned to walk away. Now I had nothing of Robinson Calculator. Not the tombstone, not my photograph. What was left?

4

Over the years, since I'd first begun looking into the Calculators, since I'd first met Lianne through Dave, I'd discovered a few places online that published various theories and speculations about the Calculators. As I waited for my Uber to take me back to the 242nd Street station, I tried to get to those sites on my phone. The little screen struggled and spun. Either the service here wasn't up to par – unlikely with four out of five bars of service – or those sites also had been eliminated.

I confirmed that when I got home, sitting near the window with a big potted snake plant and my laptop. Even the Wikipedia page on androids, which I was pretty sure had a line or two about the Calculators last time I'd looked at it, was bereft of any references to Lianne's people. Not only that, but there was no indication in the History section of the page that those lines had been removed, or had ever been there in the first place. If I correctly understood how Wikipedia worked, that must have taken some doing. More of John Calculator's intervention? This was beginning to strike me as more than the work of one man – or one Calculator. What the hell was I up against?

I sighed and shook my head. What did I have left about the Calculators? Apparently nothing.

Nothing digital, nothing carved in stone. Nothing.

That left, what?

Flesh and blood, that's what it left.

I tried Lianne again and got the same lack of result. No response in text, audio, or FaceTime.

I drummed my fingers on the table, and tried the next best. I called Dave.

"Hey Jonathan," he answered.

I exhaled with some relief. At least Dave hadn't gone incommunicado. "I've been trying to get in touch with Lianne," I got right to the point, "and no luck on FaceTime, phone, or message," I told him. "I just wanted to make sure she was all right – sorry to bother you."

"Oh, no bother at all," Dave said. "She's like that. Sometimes she just goes underground. But I spoke to her today, about three or four hours ago, and she seemed fine."

That would have been right around the time she'd texted me about meeting her and John in the Indian Road Café. "I didn't know you were back in touch with her," I said, a little more stridently than I'd intended. "Sorry, I don't mean to hold you to account about Lianne – you certainly have every right—"

"It's ok," Dave replied. "Talking to you stirred some memories, and feelings. You actually have nothing to apologize about."

"I'm glad," I said. "Hey, apropos our good conversations, you up for lunch again today? My treat."

"Love to," Dave said. "But I've got a pain-in-the-ass departmental meeting today – bane of my existence."

"Tell me about it. My sympathies," I said

"Thanks," Dave said. "And I'm tied up all day tomorrow with classes."

"No problem," I said. "I'll let you go prepare for that meeting, and we can touch base later this week for lunch."

***

I resumed my finger-drumming on the table. No Internet, no tombstone, no people I could talk to who could help me. What was the point in talking to Kathleen Harney about an outer-space origin of the Calculators when I no longer had evidence of them here on Earth? Same for the blind professor and the Golem, and Chen in Dobbs Ferry.

But I had a feeling I was overlooking something. I scrolled through my email. Nothing relevant and – ah, here it was. An email forwarded to me and everyone in our Department a week ago about the New York Public Library main branch. They were finally re-opening their massive stacks – which had been under reconstruction, and open and closed for the past few years – and Fordham University faculty had privileges.

I made sure my university ID was in my wallet, dashed out of my apartment, and fast-walked to the A train. Someone was playing the Beatles' "Helter Skelter" out of a car – the 2018 remix, which was my favorite. It seemed appropriate to how I was feeling and what I was doing today.

The subway was fast and easy. I got out at 42nd Street, and walked quickly to Fifth Avenue and those iconic lions that stood stately guard at the entrance to the library. I'd been in the stacks a few times in my life. My Uncle Morty had worked there when he was a student at City College in the 1960s. Easy train ride for him, too, 125th Street down to 42nd Street via the D train.

He'd told me all sorts of stories about the stacks. Some, about ghosts and zombies, were no doubt apocryphal. I half snickered to myself. This whole insane thing had started in a cemetery, right? A ghostly presence in the New York Public Library could fit right in.

My uncle had told me other stories, like how he'd made out with a girl in the stacks. Who knew if that was true? What I did know is that there was something otherworldly, an aura of anything could happen, in those stacks. I'd really enjoyed my few visits, though by the time I'd first arrived there, the goblins were gone. And I wasn't able to prowl the stacks directly. The best I could do was ask a page – the great name for a library assistant who wasn't a librarian or even a clerk – to see if the stacks had a book I'd needed.

The stacks were now called the Milstein Research Stacks, and in 2016 a sophisticated conveyor system had been installed by Teledynamic, a company in New Jersey. I read all about that on a plaque on the wall in the lobby of the library. It advised people who needed books in the stacks to go to the Rose Reading Room or a room on the first floor. I went to the first floor room – after all, I was on that floor right now.

There was another sign about the stacks right outside the room. They'd been expanded in new facilities under Bryant Park, right next to the library. I could make my request to a member of the "staff," who would put in my request to staff at the stacks. If the book or books I wanted were there, someone would put them on the conveyor back to this room.

I walked up to a woman who stood behind a counter. Judging by her age – which looked to be at least 75 or older – she was likely retired from whatever her life's work had been, and worked here as a volunteer. Lots of people who loved books did this.

She smiled at me and looked at my ID. "How can I assist you professor?"

"I'm researching androids – robots," I told her. "And I was wondering if you could get me the oldest book you have on the subject. Or books, if you have more than one." I'd thought this out on the train. I highly doubted there'd be a book with "Calculator" in the title – or, there were no doubt hundreds of books with the word in the title in the stacks, but they were about pocket calculators and all kinds of other calculators, not about Robinson or Lianne or John and their extended family.

The woman nodded and typed into her keyboard.

"Thank you, Ms. Lyncroft," I said, assuming she was the Davina Lyncroft whose name was on a little Victorian nameplate on her counter. It looked old, but I assumed it was a repro.

"You're very welcome, professor," she said. "This could take a few minutes. You're welcome to wait in that chair," she pointed to a plush, oversized armchair. "We have very good wifi. You don't need a password."

"Thanks, I think I will," I smiled and went to the chair. It was even more comfortable than it looked.

I scrolled through my photos, on the chance that maybe I had accidentally repositioned the photo of the tombstone, perhaps inadvertently set it to a much earlier date. Or maybe I had somehow moved it to the "Recently deleted" folder. I found nada. I noted that every other single photo on my phone was exactly where I expected it to be. It was fun looking at them, though, hundreds of them—

"I'm sorry," Ms. Lyncroft interrupted my perusing about ten minutes later. "I just received a message from the stacks. Apparently the three oldest books with 'robot' or 'android' in the title have all gone missing."

"How could be that be?" I asked, surprised, trying not show I was also ... really annoyed. More than that. "Books from the stacks are not allowed in circulation, right?"

"Indeed," Lyncroft said and nodded. "We're looking into where the books are now. Likely they were mis-shelved. I'm sorry to say that sometimes happens."

"Mis-shelved by one of the staff?" I asked. "Or is it possible that someone got into the stacks from outside?"

"Oh no, I assure you," Lyncroft replied. "The only people allowed in those stacks are staff."

"I assume tracking those books down could take some time," I said.

"I'm afraid so, yes," Lyncroft said. "Could take days, even weeks. Those stacks are *huge*. If you give me your email, I can let you know as soon as I receive more information."

I gave her one of my cards. "Thank you," I said. "One more question. Could you give me the titles of those books? And their years of first publication?" I assumed the years were in the late 1920s, or after Čapek's *R.U.R.*

"Of course," Lyncroft said. "Give me a few minutes." She walked back to her desk.

She indeed returned a few minutes later with a piece a paper. The first thing I noticed was the year after each of the three titles. They were a hundred years earlier than what I'd expected.

***

I walked out of the library, into the sunlight, partially enlightened, partially in a stupor, born of bumping into something I could barely understand. Apparently the reach of the Calculators extended from erasing photos and words on tombstones to removing books from the New York Public Library stacks. Did someone by the name of Calculator work here?

I tried to focus on something that I'd just learned. Čapek had likely not invented the term 'robot,' but picked it up from usage a hundred years earlier. Likely Mary Shelley had picked up on that same undercurrent, if that's what it was, when she wrote *Frankenstein* a little before January, 1818, when the first edition was published. Ordinarily, that in itself would have been fascinating to know.

But it was just a footnote to what was flooding my head. The Calculators had powers that far exceeded hacking my phone or sandblasting their name off a tombstone in a public cemetery. They could get into the stacks of the New York Public Library – the soul of the Library, as I'd always thought of it – and remove the very books I was seeking. All within mere hours of my meeting John in the Indian Road Café, and less than an hour from when I'd decided to request those books from the stacks.

I cleared my throat and swallowed hard. What was my next move? Fly to another big city? New York of course wasn't the only city with a world-class library. I loved the library at the British Museum every bit as much as I loved the Library that loomed majestically behind me.

I sat on a step near a stone lion. The marble guardian had failed in its task, if any part of its job had been to protect the holdings of the library. And I had an unshakeable feeling that if I flew to every stately library cathedral in this world, the results would be the same as I'd just encountered here. The books I was seeking would be unaccountably missing.

I looked at the lion and nodded goodbye. Not your fault. There were things afoot, currents at large, that surpassed the power of any stone lion, or me, to stop or even slow down.

5

There was a message on my phone waiting for me when I ascended from the subway in Inwood. It was from Lianne. My heart jumped. I was relieved.

I walked to a nearby park bench and listened. "Don't try to return this call," she said. "I'm changing my number. But I wanted to tell you that I really enjoyed myself with you last night. And I wanted to apologize for erasing the photo on your phone and where you stored it online. I ... we're very skilled at that sort of thing. And look, I'm not saying we can never be together. It's just that ... the time is not right, not right now. Maybe sometime in the future." And she actually threw me a kiss. After all of this, a kiss.

***

I sulked the next few days. I taught my classes, moped around my office, and didn't do much of anything. Dave called me on the way home.

"My schedule finally cleared up. You free for a drink this afternoon?"

"Sure," I said, and suggested the Indian Road Café, because I didn't feel like traveling.

***

I met him there an hour later. I expected him not to show, or John Calculator to be there in his stead.

Dave ordered a beer. I ordered a Turkish wine. We looked at each other and both shook our heads.

"So, I gather you've been having a tough time of it," Dave said.

"I don't think you heard that from me," I replied, though I supposed I looked and sounded plenty beleaguered.

"No, not from you," Dave said. "They're much more powerful than you'd imagine. The digital revolution played right into their hands."

"Did they help create that?" I asked.

"Maybe, possibly, who knows? But they took to it like fish to water. The Calculators are, were, already digital in some sense." Dave looked at the waiter who had arrived with our drinks. "Thank you," he said.

"Why did they put the name Robinson Calculator on that tombstone if they're so obsessed with secrecy?" I asked.

Dave took a long sip of his beer. "That's the question. Maybe to see what kind of reaction it would evoke?"

"Hmph," I said sarcastically. "Well, I guess I certainly provided them with more of an answer than they anticipated. Running around the city and Westchester, badgering everyone I could get into a conversation, to find out who the Calculators were." I almost added, and bedding Lianne, but I was able to contain myself.

"You don't know if you were the first one to see that tombstone, or how long it was there," Dave said.

I finally sipped some wine. It was good. The only comforting thing at this table. "You know, I don't recall seeing a date on the gravestone."

Dave nodded. "Well, that makes sense, I guess. If they were trying to see what kind of response that name on a tombstone would elicit, they would include as little specific information as possible.

That would encourage anyone who saw it to wonder how it fit into their world. If there was a date of death before you even were born, that might make it seem less relevant to you."

"It was sheer luck that I even saw the damned thing," I said. "If I had just looked in any other direction at that moment, I wouldn't have seen it." Sheer luck? Sheer *bad* luck would be more like it. Maybe very bad luck, because it suddenly occurred to me that since I had indeed seen it, and had been making such a big deal about it, maybe the Calculators wanted to eliminate *me*. I'd admitted to Dave that I'd even intended to make a movie about the Calculators. Was he the hit man? My brain was racing. I wondered if maybe it had been planned for me to see that tombstone – but how could the Calculators have known that I'd be at the cemetery that day?

Dave looked at me a little oddly. "Don't beat yourself up about it."

I sipped and nodded. I had to resist being paranoid. Still, I had to be extremely careful now – in everything I did, in everything I said to Dave. "Apropos your fish and water metaphor, I think I'm going to let all this be water under the bridge. Give my Calculator hunt a rest." I realized I was beginning to truly feel that if I never saw or heard the name Calculator again, that would be ok with me. Maybe I was just reacting to everything that had happened to me since that day at the cemetery, maybe my mind was just acting in its own best defense.

Dave nodded slowly. "I think that's a very good idea. Look, I was married and walked away. Your entanglement is almost entirely of your own making."

I drained my wine glass. I actually was beginning to feel a tiny bit better already. I had no idea how many Calculators there were in this world, but there couldn't be that many. I might never see another Calculator again unless I went looking for them. I looked around for our waiter to order another glass of wine.

Dave nursed his beer, smiled, and reached over to squeeze my shoulder. "It's not easy, I know. You're making the right decision."

I nodded. "I'm going to see if I can get more wine," I said. "Anything more for you?"

"I'm alright, thanks," Dave said.

I pushed my chair back, got up, and walked to the bar. Truthfully, I could still feel Lianne on top of me, I could still smell her hair, but I could get over her. I had to. I had to at least try. The movie wasn't all that important. Lianne somehow was. But I had to give forgetting her and the Calculators a shot. I had a feeling that maybe my life depended on it.

Our waiter, who had been talking to someone at the bar, turned around. "Apologies! Is there something else you wanted?"

"Yes." I told him I'd like another glass of the same wine.

"Of course!" he said. "I'll bring it right over to you."

"Thank you," I said, and started walking back to our table. It looked like Dave was talking to someone on the phone. He was nodding vigorously.

"—Oops, sorry!" I'd walked into someone, or he into me, and he was apologizing.

"It was me," I said. "I need to look where I am walking."

"No problem!" he said, and walked quickly to the door. He looked like a Kennedy, maybe JFK, if he'd lived to be 60.

I realized, after he'd left the Café, that our collision had caused him to drop something on the floor. It was right in front of me. It was a credit card.

I bent down and picked it up. The card was face down. I turned it over. The name read "Julian Calculator."

THE FOLLOWING BOOKS
BY PAUL LEVINSON ARE
AVAILABLE ON AMAZON

Nonfiction

The Soft Edge: A Natural History and Future of the Information Revolution

Digital McLuhan: A Guide to the Information Millennium

McLuhan in an Age of Social Media

Realspace: The Fate of Physical Presence in the Digital Age, On and Off Planet

New New Media

From Media Theory to Space Odyssey: Petar Jandrić interviews Paul Levinson

Cyber War and Peace

Human Replay: A Theory of the Evolution of Media, original PhD dissertation, New York University, 1979

Fake News in Real Context

Science fiction

It's Real Life: An Alternate History of The Beatles

Loose Ends (time travel) series (complete):

Loose Ends, Little Differences, Late Lessons, Last Calls

->all four stories in one book: The Loose Ends Saga

Sierra Waters (time travel) series:

The Plot to Save Socrates, Unburning Alexandria, Chronica

Phil D'Amato forensic detective series:

The Chronology Protection Case, The Silk Code, The Consciousness Plague, The Pixel Eye

Ian's Ions and Eons (three time travel novelettes)

Exo-Genetic Engineers series:

The Orchard, The Suspended Fourth

Borrowed Tides

Double Realities series: The Other Car, Extra Credit, The Wallet, The P&A

The Kid in the Video Store

Marilyn and Monet

Peter Brown Called: Tales of SciFi and Music

Urban Corridors: Fables and Gables

Nonfiction and Science Fiction

Touching the Face of the Cosmos: On the Intersection of Space Travel and Religion

an anthology of essays and science fiction stories, including a new interview with John Glenn, an essay by Guy Consolmagno, SJ (the "Pope's Astronomer"), and contributions from leading thinkers about the role of religion in space travel

***

Interested in occasional announcements about my books?

Follow me on X/Twitter: @PaulLev

***

ABOUT THE AUTHOR

Paul Levinson

 Paul Levinson, PhD, is Professor of Communication & Media Studies at Fordham University in NYC. His nonfiction books, including The Soft Edge (1997), Digital McLuhan (1999), Realspace (2003), Cellphone (2004), and New New Media (2009; 2nd edition, 2012), have been translated into fifteen languages. His science fiction novels include The Silk Code (winner of Locus Award for Best First Science Fiction Novel of 1999), Borrowed Tides (2001), The Consciousness Plague (2002), The Pixel Eye (2003), The Plot To Save Socrates (2006), Unburning Alexandria (2013), Chronica (2014), and It's Real Life: An Alternate History of The Beatles (2024). His novelette, "The Chronology Protection Case," was made into a short movie available on Amazon Prime. His alternate history story about The Beatles, "It's Real Life," was made into a radio play available on Audible, won the Mary Shelley Award for Outstanding Fiction in 2023, and was expanded into a novel published in 2024. . He appears on CNN, MSNBC, the Discovery Channel, National Geographic, the History Channel, NPR, and numerous TV and radio programs. His 1972 LP, Twice Upon a Rhyme, was re-issued in 2010; his new LP, Welcome Up: Songs of Space and Time, was released on Old Bear Records and Light in the Attic Records in 2020. He reviews television in his InfiniteRegress.tv blog.

www.ingramcontent.com/pod-product-compliance
Lightning Source LLC
Chambersburg PA
CBHW032113170626
46808CB00008B/3045